Classic Adventures

The Adventures of Huckleberry Finn

by
Mark Twain

retold by
John Matern

Don Johnston Incorporated
Volo, Illinois

Edited by:
Jerry Stemach, MS, CCC-SLP
AAC Specialist, Adaptive Technology Center, Sonoma County, California

Gail Portnuff Venable, MS, CCC-SLP
Speech-Language Pathologist, Scottish Rite Center for Childhood Language Disorders, San Francisco, California

Dorothy Tyack, MA
Learning Disabilities Specialist, Scottish Rite Center for Childhood Language Disorders, San Francisco, California

Ted S. Hasselbring, PhD
Professor of Special Education, Vanderbilt University, Nashville, Tennessee

Cover Design and Illustration:
Karyl Shields, Joe Schwajkowski

Interior Illustrations:
Joe Schwajkowski

Published by:

Don Johnston Incorporated
26799 West Commerce Drive
DON JOHNSTON **Volo, IL 60073**

International Standard Book Number
ISBN 1-893376-05-02

Contents

Chapter 1

Huck Tricks Pap

My name is Huck Finn. You might
know me from "The Adventures of
Tom Sawyer." I am Tom's best friend.
We've had some wild times together.
In fact, last year we found a treasure
chest full of gold. It was worth twelve
thousand dollars. Me and Tom split it.
We each got six thousand dollars.
I gave my money to Judge Thatcher.
I asked him to keep it for me.

My dad is the town drunk. I call him
Pap. Pap spends all of his money on
whiskey. I don't live with him.
I live with the Widow Douglas.

In fact, last year we found a treasure chest full of gold.

She treats me like her own son.

She buys me clothes and feeds me.

The Widow Douglas is always teaching

me, too. She says I need to learn my

manners. She also wants me to pray.

But I don't know about that God stuff.

I try to pray, but it doesn't work.

I figure that if praying worked,

everybody would be happy.

But they ain't happy.

     The Widow Douglas also put me in

school. She says that all boys should

know how to read and write.

I know how to read. And I can write.

She says I need to learn my manners.

I am learning math, too. I can multiply any number up to six. I like school. I like the Widow Douglas, too. I am happy here, but I get bored. This is why I like Tom Sawyer.

At night, Tom comes over to my house to get me. I sneak out of my window. We have adventures all night long. One night, Tom started a gang. I joined it. Other kids joined it, too. Tom wanted his gang to be like the famous gangs. The people in those gangs were real bandits. They had guns and knives.

We have adventures all night long.

We don't have guns or knives. We use sticks and brooms. Tom says that they are just as good. The famous gangs robbed people and killed people. Sometimes, they kidnapped people. They would hold those people for "ransom." We don't know what "ransom" means, but Tom reckons we should do it anyway.

Our gang had adventures all summer long. Then winter came. Snow was all over the ground. One morning, I found footprints in the snow.

"Did you come to get some money?" asked the judge.

I followed them. The footprints went
around to the back of my house.
I knew that Pap had made those
footprints. He wanted my money.
I didn't want to give my money to Pap,
so I ran to Judge Thatcher's house.

"Did you come to get some money?"
asked the judge.

"I don't want my money. I don't want
any of it," I said.

"What do you mean?" asked the
judge.

That's when I saw the man sitting in my room.

"I mean that I don't ever want my money. I don't ever want it back," I told him.

"What?" asked the judge. "Do you want to sell me your money?"

"Fine," I said, "I just don't want it."

The judge wrote something on a piece of paper and I signed it. I sold all of my money to the judge for one dollar. After that I went home. I snuck into my room and lit a candle. That's when I saw the man sitting in my room. It was my old Pap. He was plenty mad at me and he wanted my money.

Chapter 2

Pap's Cabin

Pap laid into me good. He didn't like my fancy clothes. Pap hated school, too. He didn't want me to go to school anymore. But Pap was the maddest about the money. He said that my money was his money since he was my dad. I told him that I gave my money to the judge. Pap was so mad that he decided to take me with him right then and there. He took me out to his cabin in the woods.

I lived in that cabin for a while. Me and Pap would go fishing in the Mississippi River every day.

I lived in that cabin for a while.

Then we would eat fish for breakfast.

When Pap went into town, he would

lock me up inside the cabin. He didn't

want me to run away. I didn't mind

much, except when Pap got drunk.

When Pap drank whiskey, he would

go crazy. He would yell and scream

all kinds of stuff. Sometimes he would

even try to hit me. One time Pap really

did hit me. That's when I decided to

leave.

One day I waited until Pap was in

town. Then I broke out of the cabin.

I could have just ran away, but I didn't want Pap to follow me. I wanted him to think that I was dead so he would never bother me again. After I snuck out, I came back and broke down the door of the cabin. I made it look like robbers came and killed me. I took everything out of the cabin. Then I killed a pig. I smeared the pig's blood all over the floor of pap's cabin. When I was done, I found a canoe and paddled down the river. I was free at last.

When I was done, I found a canoe and paddled

down the river.

I paddled all the way down to

Jackson Island. When I got there,

I sure was tired. I pulled the canoe up

on shore and fell asleep right away.

I didn't wake up 'til the next morning.

I went fishing and had fish for

breakfast, just like me and Pap always

did. Then I went exploring. I wanted

to see if anyone else was on the island.

I walked around for a while until I saw

smoke. Smoke meant that somebody

had made a fire. I wasn't alone on

Jackson Island.

I went fishing and had fish for breakfast, just like me and Pap always did.

I wanted to find out who was living
on the island. So I went to the place
where the fire was. There was a man
sleeping by the fire. And who do you
think it was? It was old Jim. He was
the Widow Douglas' slave. I knew
Jim from when I lived with the widow.
Jim and me were good friends.

I woke Jim up. "Hello there, Jim,"
I said. I was plenty happy to see him.

"Oh no," Jim said, "Now, now... you
ghost! Just leave me be. I ain't done
nothin' to you."

"Hello there, Jim," I said.

Poor old Jim thought that I was a ghost.

"I'm not a ghost," I told him. "It's me, Huck Finn." Well, it took a while, but at last old Jim believed me. Then Jim told me that he was running away from the Widow Douglas. She was fixin' to sell him to a man in New Orleans. If that happened, Jim would never see his family again. Me and Jim talked and talked. Jim's a funny old man.

Chapter 3

The Storm

From then on, me and Jim were a team. We liked to explore together. We found our own food, like wild grapes and strawberries. One day we found a cave on the top of a big hill. Jim said that we should move all our stuff into that cave because he was sure that it was going to rain soon. So we moved all our stuff up there and sure enough, it rained. It rained and rained. It rained for two weeks.

It rained so much that the river grew big and wide. It grew so much that it came up to our cave.

Sometimes old rafts or canoes would float by. We grabbed one raft as it floated past us. It was real big and we knew that we could use it. One time a whole house floated by. That was just too much. Me and Jim had to see what was in that house. So we swam out to it and looked inside. There wasn't that much in the house. We took some old clothes and a lantern. Then Jim found a dead body in the house! I wanted to see it, but Jim wouldn't let me.

Sometimes old rafts or canoes would float by.

He said that a dead body was too scary. I knew that it would not scare me, but I didn't argue with Jim.

I started to get bored on the island after three weeks. I wanted to know if Pap was still looking for me, so I decided to go to shore and ask about him. Jim was afraid that someone would remember me and tell on me. So we made a plan to dress me up like a girl. We found a dress and hat and I put them on. Then I paddled the canoe to shore.

Then Jim found a dead body in the house!

I went up to the first house that I saw and knocked on the door.

A nice old lady opened the door and asked me to come inside. We sat down and talked for a while. Then I asked her, "Have you heard about Huck Finn?"

"Well, of course I have. Everyone has heard about Huck Finn," she said. I hoped that she would tell me about Pap.

"Do they know who killed Huck?" I asked.

"Well, at first they thought that old Pap Finn done it himself," the lady told me. "They thought that Pap had killed his own son. But now they think that a runaway slave named Jim killed Huck because Jim disappeared on the same night."

This was bad news for poor Jim. "Jim is not a slave," I said.

"Yes, he is a slave" said the old lady. "My husband thinks that Jim is hiding out on Jackson Island. My husband is going over there tonight to catch him." Well, I just about lost my head.

I got out of there as fast as I could.
I ran back to my canoe and paddled
out to the island. I got Jim. We
grabbed some stuff and we left quick.
I was in the canoe, and Jim was on
the raft.

We floated on the river at night, so
that nobody would see Jim. We would
wait 'til dark and then float all night.
When the sun came up in the morning,
we would pull ashore. First we would
hide our raft, then we would eat and
talk.

We would wait 'til dark and then float all night.

Sometimes we would take food from a farmer and eat it. We reckoned that we weren't stealing. We were just borrowing. My Pap always said that it was OK to borrow things if you really needed them.

Chapter 4

Huck and Jim Get Split Up

Me and Jim just kept on floating down that river. We reckoned that we would float down to the place where the Ohio River came into the Mississippi. Jim could take the Ohio River to the North and be a free man. I was not supposed to take a slave to freedom, but Jim was my friend, and I just couldn't help it.

One night we floated into some thick fog. I tried to paddle ahead in the canoe to look around. I couldn't see a thing.

Then I tried to go back to the raft, but
I couldn't see a thing there either.
I couldn't even find Jim and the raft.
We both started yelling and whooping.
I could hear old Jim, but I couldn't see
him. We kept on like that most of the
night. Finally I couldn't even hear Jim
anymore. I figured that he got lost in
the fog.

When the sun came up, I could see
again. I pulled my canoe ashore.
I looked for Jim and the raft, but I still
couldn't find him.

So I just walked along the shore until I come upon a big log house. When I got there, about a hundred dogs come running out at me. They got in a circle around me and started barking. I froze.

"Are you a Shepard?" a man yelled from the house.

"No sir," I yelled back, "It's just me."

"Who are you?" he asked. "You sure you ain't a Shepard?"

"Yes sir," I yelled. "I'm just a boy. I'm George Jackson." I made up a name.

When I got there, about a hundred dogs come

running out at me.

When they were sure that I wasn't from the Shepard family, they brought me into the house. They turned out to be right nice people.

They were the Granger family. There was a husband and wife, two girls, and three boys. And they were all beautiful. The Granger family hated the Shepard family. They had been at war with each other for a very long time. They didn't even remember who started the war.

Buck was one of the boys.

He was my age, so me and him played together that day. He took me out hunting. He wasn't hunting for animals, though. He was hunting for Shepards. And he almost got one, too. We saw Harvey Shepard riding his horse, and Buck shot the hat right off Harvey's head. Buck told his father later, and his father got mad. Mr. Granger said that Buck should not have missed.

The next morning I woke up late and nobody was in the house. I asked one of the slaves where everyone was.

We saw Harvey Shepard riding his horse, and Buck

shot the hat right off Harvey's head.

The slave told me that one of Mr.
Granger's daughters had snuck out
that night. She had fallen in love with
Harvey Shepard, and they left to get
married. The rest of the family had
found out and went to kill Harvey.
I thought Buck might need my help,
so I went to find him.

I heard gunshots all over the place.
I walked toward the shots to find Buck.
When I got there, I climbed a tree so
I could see everything. There was
Buck, behind a rock with another boy.

When I got there, I climbed a tree so I could see

everything.

And he was shooting away at those Shepards. But then the Shepards snuck up behind Buck and shot him dead. There was nothing I could do. I waited until the fighting was over. Then I walked down to the river. Who do you think was waiting for me? Old Jim, that's who. We hopped back on the raft and floated out of there.

Chapter 5

The King and Duke

It was nice to be back on the river with Jim. It turns out that he was at the Granger's house, too. He stayed with the slaves there. The slaves told him that I left to find Buck and never came back. Poor old Jim thought that I was dead again. We were happy to be back together. At night, we laid on our backs and looked up into the sky. We talked about how the stars got up there. Jim said that the moon laid the stars. I've seen frogs lay about that many eggs, so I didn't argue.

One night, we saw two men running to the river. They said that they were being chased and they needed our help. We let them get on our raft. These two men were something else. They said that they were being chased for no reason at all. They said that they hadn't done nothing wrong.

Well, I didn't believe that, but I let them stay on the raft. Later, one of the men says to us, "What a pity. I'm stuck on this raft when I should be in a castle."

"What are you talking about?" I asked him.

"I'm a king," he said. "But I have had bad luck and now I'm stuck on this raft." Well, when Jim heard this he just about went crazy. Jim started calling the man "sir" and running all over the raft trying to please him. Jim gave him his bed and made all his food for him.

When the other man saw all this, he looked real sad and said, "I know how you feel, King. I was once a Duke." So this man tells the same story. And Jim started serving both of them.

I was pretty sure that they were
pulling our leg, but I didn't say nothin'.
Everyone seemed happy this way.
I didn't want to cause no trouble.

After a few days, the King and the
Duke wanted to stop. They said they
wanted to do a play for the people in
the next town. So we stopped at the
next town. I went into town with the
King and Duke, but Jim had to stay
on the raft. The play was called "The
Royal Nonesuch." The King and Duke
put posters up all over town.

The King and Duke put posters up all over town.

The posters said that the play was famous all over the world and that the King and Duke were famous actors.

On the first night, about half the town came to the play. We charged them all fifty cents to see it. Well, it wasn't much to see. When the Duke lifted the curtain, there was the King. And he was naked and covered in paint! The King rolled around and yelled and screamed all sorts of stuff. The crowd laughed and laughed. Then the Duke dropped the curtain and that was all.

And he was naked and covered in paint!

Let me tell you, the crowd was plenty
mad. But they didn't say nothin'.
They didn't want the rest of the town
to know that they had been suckered.

So the King and Duke did the same
thing the next night. And there were
even more people there. When that
show ended, that crowd was mad, too.
But they didn't say nothin' either.
So the King and Duke decided to put
the play on again the next night.
This time the whole town showed up.
And they was all carrying stuff in their
pants and coats.

Then the King and Duke counted their money.

Some people had rotten apples. Other people had smelly eggs. After they all paid to get in, I went and told the Duke. Well, he didn't even lift the curtain this time. The three of us ran for our lives. Jim was waiting on the raft for us. We all got on and headed down the river. Then the King and Duke counted their money. They had made 465 dollars on that silly play.

Chapter 6

The Wilks Scandal

We all hid after that for a while. The four of us just kept on floating down that river. Soon enough, though, the King was making a new plan to cheat someone. We came across a man who wanted to get on a steamboat. The man asked if the King was Mr. Wilks, from England. The King said no, but then offered the man a ride on the raft to the steamboat. On the way to the steamboat, the King asked the man all sorts of questions. I could tell the King was up to no good.

The King asked all about the Wilks family. We found out that a man named Peter Wilks had just died. Peter's brothers were coming from England to read Peter's will. Right then I knew what the King was planning to do.

The King went and got the Duke. The King told the Duke the whole story about the Wilks family. One of Peter's brothers was deaf and couldn't talk, either. The Duke would pretend to be the deaf brother.

When the King and Duke were ready, the three of us

went into town.

The King practiced talking like someone from England. I would be their servant. When the King and Duke were ready, the three of us went into town. Jim had to wait on the raft again.

The King walked up to the first person he saw. "Excuse me," he said. "Could you tell me where my dear brother, Peter, lived?"

Well, that person got excited and asked, "Is it you? Are you Peter's dear brother from England?"

"I am indeed," the King said. Then the King started crying. Then the King looked at the Duke and the Duke cried, too. Soon, the whole town had come to see us. They were happy to see us. Peter's daughters even came and kissed the King and Duke. Then they took us to their house.

The King was sure a good actor. He could answer all the people's questions. Just from what he heard from the man going to the steamboat. The Duke just made "goo goo" noises and followed the King around.

Peter's daughters were really nice. There were three daughters. They were as sweet as can be. I started to feel bad for those three daughters.

Soon, the daughters gave Peter's will to the King and Duke. The will told them where Peter hid all his money. Peter had saved up six thousand dollars. He wanted his daughters to share his money. But the King and Duke hid the money in their room. They weren't going to share it with anyone. That wasn't all, either.

Soon, the daughters gave Peter's will to the King and

Duke.

The King and Duke planned to sell the house and keep that money, too. That was more than I could take.

When everyone was asleep that night, I snuck into the King's room. I snuck the money out of his room and took it downstairs. I wanted to hide it outside somewhere. Then later I could tell the daughters where it was hid. Well, I was almost outside when Mary, Peter's daughter, came down the stairs. I didn't have time to get outside.

I snuck the money out of his room and took it

downstairs.

If she saw me, she would think I was robbing her. I had to hide the money fast. Peter's coffin was the only thing in the room. So I put the money in the coffin and ran back upstairs.

68

Chapter 7

The Real Wilks

The King and Duke woke me up the next morning. They were fighting and yelling at each other. They knew their money was gone. They asked me if I took it and I said of course not. I told them that I didn't know what they were talking about. It took a while, but they believed me. They figured they would still sell the house, anyway. At least they would get some money.

Well the King and the Duke had a big auction. The King was up there selling everything in sight.

He sold the slaves, the chairs, and even the pots and pans. He was selling stuff cheap, too. He didn't have time to sell the house, though. Before he got to the house, the real Wilks brothers showed up. Sure enough, one of them couldn't talk and the other one could. The one who couldn't talk had a cast on his arm. I thought we were done for sure this time. But the King didn't give up. The King called the Wilks brothers fakes. The King just wouldn't quit! Well, the people in the town got confused.

They didn't know who to believe.
Then one of them got an idea.

The people decided to have a
handwriting contest. They told the
King and the Wilks brother to each
write a sentence. So the King and
the Wilks brother each wrote a
sentence. Then the people
compared the sentences to a real
letter from Peter's brother. Nothing
matched! The Duke tried to write a
sentence, but he was just as bad.

And since the brother with the cast couldn't write at all, the people in the town had to think of another test.

Then the real Wilks brother says, "I can solve this once and for all. Peter had a tattoo on his chest. Why don't we see who can describe it?" But did the King give up? No sir.

"The tattoo is a blue arrow," the King said. "It is very small and hard to see."

"Here you are wrong," said the Wilks brother.

"The tattoo is P-M-B, Peter's initials."

But the King still didn't give up.

"You say it is P-M-B," said the King. "And I say it is an arrow. We will never know who is right. The body is already buried." My goodness, the King was smart. But that didn't even work. The people got mad and decided to dig up Peter's body. They were going to settle this for sure.

So the whole town went running out to the graveyard. Poor old Peter had been buried only a couple of hours. Now they was digging him up again.

Well, they dug up the coffin and you know what

they found?

They locked up the King and Duke while they dug up Peter. One of the men held me by the arm. Well, they dug up the coffin and you know what they found? Yes, all the money. The whole town went crazy. Everyone rushed in to see the money. I didn't stick around to see what happened next. The man who was holding me forgot all about me. As soon as he let go of my arm, I took off. I ran all the way to the raft. I found the raft, but old Jim wasn't there.

I found the raft, but old Jim wasn't there.

I looked everywhere, but I couldn't find him. I figured somebody must have found him and turned him in. Well, me and Jim had been through too much. I decided right then that I would find Jim and set him free again. After all, we was friends.

Chapter 8

Huck and Tom Again

I asked the first boy I saw if he had
seen any runaway slaves. The boy
said, yes, somebody had just found
a runaway slave on a raft. He
described the slave, and I knew it
was Jim. The boy told me that Jim
had been taken down the river. A man
named Silas Phelps was keeping Jim.
I thanked the boy and went straight to
the Phelps' house. I found their house
and I just walked right up to the door.
I didn't know what I was going to say.

She took me inside and fussed over me.

I always thought of something, though. This time I didn't have to think at all.

A lady saw me coming and ran out of the house to meet me. "Is that you, Tom?" she asked. There was only one answer to that.

"Yes ma'am," I said. She took me inside and fussed over me. She said that she was expecting me. That lady talked and talked. I nodded my head and tried to think of a plan. I ran out of time, though.

"So, tell me all about your family, Tom," she said. I was stuck. I figured that I would have to tell her the truth. But then a man walked through the door. The lady jumped up and shouted, "Silas, look who's here. It's Tom Sawyer!"

I just about fell over. They thought I was their nephew, Tom Sawyer. This lady was Tom's aunt and this man was Tom's uncle! It was my lucky day. I talked up a storm, now. I knew all about Tom's family.

I called the lady and the man Aunt Sally and Uncle Silas. I had a great time. Then it hit me. What if Tom really did show up? I would have to meet him before he got here. If he came now, he would spoil my whole plan. I told Aunt Sally and Uncle Silas that I left my bags at the dock. I said I wanted to get them before dark. I left to find Tom.

Just a mile down the road was Tom Sawyer. He was plenty surprised to see me, too.

He turned white and said, "I ain't never hurt a dead

person.

He turned white and said, "I ain't never hurt a dead person. You ghosts just leave me alone!" I got a good laugh at Tom. Then I told him the whole story. I told him how I tricked Pap. I told how me and Jim was floatin' down the river ever since. Then I told him how his aunt and uncle thought that I was Tom Sawyer.

This was the kind of stuff that Tom loved. He asked me all about my adventures.

Tom decided that he would pretend to be Sid.

Then he told me that he would think of a plan to fool his aunt and uncle. Tom decided that he would pretend to be Sid. Sid was Tom's brother. Well Tom's plan worked great. We both stayed with Aunt Sally and Uncle Silas, and they believed us.

Once we got settled, we started thinking of how we would free Jim. My idea was to sneak Jim out the window at night. Tom said that my idea would work but that it was no good.

It was too easy. Tom said that a good plan had to be dangerous. Well Tom came up with a good plan all right. It would work. Plus it had a good chance of getting us all killed.

Chapter 9

Getting Ready

We found out quickly where Silas was keeping Jim. Silas kept bringing plates full of food to the shed out back. Then the plates came back empty. We figured that a shed didn't eat that much food, so it must be Jim inside that shed. Poor old Jim was locked in a shed out back. Me and Tom went to work on the plan.

I thought we should use a shovel to dig Jim out. Tom said that nobody ever escaped that way. It was too easy. Tom said we needed to dig with spoons. So we tried.

I thought we should use a shovel to dig Jim out.

We dug and dug all night. Our hands hurt, but we didn't even make a hole. Tom decided we could use a shovel and pretend that it was a spoon. When the hole was dug, I thought we was ready. Tom said we wasn't ready yet.

"Huck," he said, "We can't just have him slip out the hole. There are things we need to do first."

"We dug the hole," I said. "What else?"

"Huck, you make everything too simple. If this is going to be a real escape, then we'll need to do more," Tom answered.

"Fine," I said. "Let's make it a real escape. What else do we need to do?" Well, it turned out we needed to do a lot more.

First, Tom said we needed to get a rope. Then we had to sneak it in to Jim. I told Tom that we weren't going to use it. Tom said that wasn't the point. Then Tom said that Jim needed to have pets.

So me and Tom caught a bunch of rats and snakes.

All the famous people who escaped had pets. So me and Tom caught a bunch of rats and snakes. Jim didn't want them, but we put them in his shed anyway. Tom also told us that Jim had to have a plant. Jim said that he didn't have any water for the plant. Tom told Jim that he had to cry and water the plant with his tears. Old Jim couldn't cry enough to keep the plant alive. So Tom gave him an onion. Every day, Jim would smell that onion, start to cry, and then water his plant.

Every day, Jim would smell that onion, start to cry, and then water his plant.

Then Tom said that Jim had to write down his plan in blood. Well, Jim didn't know how to write. Tom told him to just scribble on the floor.

Jim went along with it. Every time a rat bit him, he would scribble on the floor with his blood. It took us about a week, but at last Tom was happy.

The last thing we needed was to write a note. The note was to warn everybody that Jim was going to escape. Now this didn't make any sense to me.

"Why do we want to warn people that Jim is escaping?" I asked.

"How will anybody know that Jim is escaping if we don't tell them?" he asked me back.

"Nobody will know," I told Tom. "But isn't that the idea?" I said.

"If nobody knows," Tom said, "then nobody will try to stop us. That's not exciting. That's not adventure. It would be too easy," Tom said.

So we wrote the note.

It said:

Dear Sir,

A gang of Indians is planning to steal your slave tonight. They will be here at midnight. Try to stop them...

We put the note on the door that night and went off to bed.

Chapter 10

The Escape

Me and Tom waited up late that night. All sorts of people came over to the house. I guess Silas got pretty scared by the note. He called most of the town over to help catch the Indians. This was just what Tom wanted. Just before midnight, me and Tom snuck out the window and went out to the shed. We snuck in through our hole and got Jim ready. Before we could get out, someone opened the door to the shed.

It was dark in there, so they couldn't see us. We all slipped out the hole right before they lit the lantern.

We ran all the way to the fence at the edge of the field. Jim jumped over it. Then I hopped over it, too. But Tom got his coat stuck on the fence post. Everybody heard his coat tear on the post, and they were after us. Then they started shooting their guns at us. I don't know how, but we all got down to the raft. Me and Jim were plenty happy to make it. Tom was even happier.

Tom had been shot in the leg. Just like a real escape.

"Go on, go on!" yelled Tom. "I'll be OK."

Jim looked at me and said, "Now do you think that Master Tom would go on if we's been shot? No Sirree, he wouldn't. And so's neither will I." Jim sat down and waited. I agreed. We needed to get a doctor for Tom. We decided that I would fetch the doctor, and Jim would stay with Tom. So I walked back into town and ran smack dab into Silas.

And he was carrying Tom.

I didn't have time to get a doctor or anything else. Uncle Silas took me straight home and sat me with Aunt Sally. She didn't let me out of her sight.

The next morning Tom still wasn't home. We waited around all day, but he still didn't show up. I was just itchin' to go get him, but Aunt Sally wouldn't let me. Everyone got plenty worried that day. Finally, that night someone come to the door. It was old Jim. And he was carrying Tom. There was a real ruckus then.

Aunt Sally put Tom in bed and locked
Jim up. They thought that Jim had
kidnapped Tom. Uncle Silas called
the doctor and he came right over.
I couldn't talk to Tom or Jim.

The next morning I snuck into Tom's
room real early. But Aunt Sally came
in right behind me. Then Tom woke
up and started talking.

"Aunt Sally? Huck? Did we do it?
Did we set old Jim free?"

"Who's Huck?" asked Aunt Sally.
"And what's all this slave stuff?"

I had to tell him that Jim got caught.

Aunt Sally was mighty confused.
Then Tom just up and told the whole
story. He told her everything! He
told her how we had tricked her
and Uncle Silas. He told her how
we tried to free Jim. I couldn't
believe it. I had to tell him that Jim
got caught. Tom sat straight up in
bed.

"Jim can't be caught. Jim's a free
man. The old Widow Douglas died.
She set Jim free when she died,"
he said.

Jim was very happy.

"So why did you want to set him free if he was already free?" I asked.

Tom smiled and said, "For the adventure, Huck."

I went and told Jim. Jim was very happy. Then he told me I was free, too. That dead man in the floating house was my Pap. He would never bother me again. Well, I guess that now we were all happy. And we figured Tom was right. That was some adventure.

The End

112

A Note from the Start-to-Finish Editors

This book has been divided into approximately equal short chapters so that the student can read a chapter and take the cloze test in one reading session. This length constraint has sometimes required the authors to make transitions in mid-chapter or to break up chapters in unexpected places.

Some content change is inevitable in order to retell a 400-page book in less than 8000 words. The authors have had to eliminate some characters and incidents and sometimes manipulate the story's sequence to produce a cohesive story. Every attempt has been made to maintain the essence of the plot, characters, and style of the book.

You will also notice that Start-to-Finish Books look different from other high-low readers and chapter books. The text layout of this book coordinates with the other media components (CD and audio-cassette) of the Start-to-Finish series.

The text in the book matches, line-for-line and page-for-page, the text shown on the computer screen, enabling readers to follow along easily in the book. Each page ends in a complete sentence so that the student can either practice the page (repeat reading) or turn the page to continue with the story. If the next sentence cannot fit on the page in its entirety, it has been shifted to the next page. For this reason, the sentence at the top of a page may not be indented, signaling that it is part of the paragraph from the preceding page.

Words are not hyphenated at the ends of lines. This sometimes creates extra space at the end of a line, but eliminates confusion for the struggling reader.